Estrella, Shining Brightly

by Anne Sibley O'Brien
illustrated by Melanie Hall

Chapters

In Mexico	2
To California	6
The Movies	12

Harcourt

Orlando   Boston   Dallas   Chicago   San Diego

Visit *The Learning Site!*

www.harcourtschool.com

In Mexico

As long as I can remember, Papa has been a painter and a dreamer. When I was little, he worked as a mural painter in Mexico. Mama would sometimes take me with her when she visited him on the job, and we would sing songs all the way. When Papa saw us, he would climb off the high wooden platform, hold out his arms, and call, "Estrella! My little star! Give me a smile!" I would run to him, and he would swing me up, up into the air.

Then came the revolution, with soldiers and the sounds of guns. From day to day, Papa did not know whether there would be work for him. Finally, he decided he must go to California to find a safe place for our family. The day he left, I could see the fear in Mama's eyes.

"I will make a way for us," he said, kissing Mama good-bye. His voice was full of determination, though his eyes were sad. He knelt down, looked into my eyes, and said, "Shine brightly, little star. Be good company to your Mama and the little ones. I will send for you soon!"

A long, long waiting time followed. Mama worked very hard, but she never sang anymore. Neighbors gave her condolences, as if my father were gone forever instead of just gone to look for a new home. I tried hard to be helpful and shine brightly for Mama. I played games with Alberto and Rosita. They were the same games Papa used to play with me.

When I tried to be a scary bear or a galloping horse, my brother and sister were confused. "Estrella," Alberto said one day, "I don't like you to be the bear. I want to play scary bear with Papa!"

In California, Papa got work picking lemons, moving from place to place. Then he got work on the railroad, still moving.

In Mexico, the shooting continued in the streets. At night, I looked at the stars and hoped they were shining down on my father, too. Finally, a letter came saying Papa had found work painting. He described the small house he had found for us. It was time for us to move to California, he said. That was the day Mama began singing again.

To California

We rode on the train for days, a train that was crowded with people also looking for a safe home. I told every story I knew to keep Alberto and Rosita from fussing. When I wasn't telling them stories, Mama sang quietly to them. She sang happy songs and silly songs and even a few sad songs.

When the little ones finally fell asleep, Mama and I stared out the window. I was amazed to see how big and beautiful Mexico was! There were places of green hills and trees, places of dry, brown sand, and places of steep mountains that plunged to the sea. We felt sad to be leaving, sad about the fighting, but so happy to be joining Papa.

When we got near the northern edge of Mexico, the train stopped, and we walked to the border. Many other Mexicans walked with us. It was hot, and we were thirsty. At the gate, Mama had to sign a paper and pay a tax. Then we walked across the border, and we were in California! I was surprised to see that it looked just like parts of Mexico.

We walked and walked until we boarded another train to take us to a place called Los Angeles, our new home.

When we got off the train, Papa was waiting. First, he hugged and kissed Mama, Alberto, and Rosita. Then, he held out his arms and called, "Estrella! My little star! Give me a smile!" I couldn't stop smiling all day. I smiled so much my cheeks hurt!

All around us at the station were people who were talking and shouting, but I couldn't understand a word they said. We took a trolley car to our new home in the barrio; there, children called to each other in Spanish, just as they had in Mexico. *Everything is going to be fine here,* I told myself. Then Papa pointed across a ravine to a low, white building. It was my new school.

I started school the very next day. Everything felt strange. I couldn't read anything the teacher wrote on the board, and I couldn't understand a single word she said. After that first morning, it was hard to go to school every day. When I felt sad, I would think about what my father said to me each morning: "Shine brightly today, my little star!" So I copied down the letters from the board, repeated the words the teacher said, and wondered whether I would ever understand English.

At night, I sat outside and looked at the stars. They looked just like the stars in Mexico, but they didn't seem to be shining on me. Instead, they seemed to be strange and mocking, like everything else in my new country. In the morning, even the smell of Mama's tortillas and the sound of her singing didn't cheer me.

Then one day, I understood one or two words the teacher said. I listened carefully, and three or four more words made sense. I was beginning to learn English!

When summer vacation came, Papa said I could visit him at his job. "Estrella, you have been working so hard at your studies that you haven't had time to smile," he said. "I work in a place of lights and dreams. I will take you there tomorrow. You will see that anything can happen! It is a magic place. Maybe we can find your smile there." I could not imagine such a place, but I was glad to spend time with my father.

The Movies

Papa's job was painting background scenery for a company that made movies. From the outside, the windowless building of the movie company looked very plain. Inside, though, there was a world of magic, just as Papa had promised.

There were whole streets full of buildings, scenes of tall mountains and waterfalls, and even a picture of an enormous sky full of storm clouds. When you walked behind the scenery, there was nothing but a flat wall of wood.

"The actors act out the story in front of my scenery," Papa explained. "The camera takes moving pictures of everything they do. When you see the

movie in a theater, the background scenery looks like a real city or a real sky."

Papa showed me the scenery that he and the other painters had finished. Then I was allowed to watch the moviemaking with him as long as I was very quiet. I watched the actors talk and move in rooms that weren't really rooms. Bright lights shone down while the cameras followed them.

Papa pointed to a tall older man who was telling everyone what to do. "That's the director," he said. "He asks the actors to say the same things over and over until the scene is perfect."

As Papa and I stood watching, the director came over and said, "Hello. I am very glad to meet one of our scenery painters and his daughter."

Papa shook the director's hand. "I am Francisco Gonzalez," he said.

Then Papa glanced at me, and I said clearly, "My name is Estrella," just as they taught us in school.

"Well, Estrella," said the director. "Would you like to be in my movie, if we have your father's approval, of course?" I squeezed Papa's hand so he would know I wanted to say yes.

"We would be honored," said Papa.

The director said, "Estrella, I'd like you to be an extra. You'll be in the background of the movie. Do you think you could follow my directions?"

"Yes!" I said.

So for five days I went to work with my father because I was going to work, too. It wasn't easy being an extra. There was a lot of waiting for costumes, for makeup, and for the cameras. We practiced my scene over and over.

SCENE 23
TAKE 2

Months later, my movie came to a theater down-
town. All five of us put on our best clothes and
went to see it. In the movie, a handsome man is
enchanted with a beautiful singer and goes to a
fancy hall to hear her sing. After the concert, the
handsome man and beautiful woman walk down a
street, laughing and singing. Then they pass by a
charming little house.

The man and woman notice a girl leaning out the first-floor window of the house. Below the window is a window box full of flowers, and the girl is watering them. The camera comes in close and shows the girl's face.

It's me! There I am—the girl in the window! I notice the man and the woman, and I see how happy they are. I pick one of the flowers and hand it to the beautiful singer.

For just a moment, the camera catches me there, holding a flower. I am shining brightly, Papa's little star. I smile for all the world to see.